To Andrew,
Enjoy!

Barbie Bettenberg

To Andrew,
Enjoy!

Leslie Ballentine

Edgar, The Near-Sighted Eagle

WRITTEN BY BARBIE BETTENBERG

ILLUSTRATED BY MARILYN CLEMENT

Published by Cricket XPress of MN
504 Bluebird Court
Sartell, MN 56377

Text by Barbie Bettenberg
Illustrations by Marilyn Clement
Cover Design by Marilyn Clement

Printed in the United States

Library of Congress Cataloging-in-Publication Data
Bettenberg, Barbie
    Edgar, The Near-Sighted Eagle/Barbie Bettenberg
    - illustrated by Marilyn Clement
Summary: Some of us are born with flaws... Edgar's problem with his
          sight is corrected with a little help from his friends.

ISBN# 978-0-9822534-0-3

This book is dedicated to two
very special little people.

CHASE AND CARMEN

You are my inspiration.

Edgar, Ernie and Ethel are sitting in their nest waiting for Mother Eagle to come home.

"Is that Mother?" cried Edgar, pointing.

"No, you silly," said Ethel kindly. "That's just a kite."

"You sure can't see well for an eagle," grumbled Ernie. "I can see a mouse from a long ways off," he boasted.

"Leave him alone!" said Ethel. "Edgar's a wonderful eagle! It's not his fault he can't see well."

"That's right," cooed Mother Eagle as she glided into the nest. "Edgar's vision will get better as he gets older. You wait and see. Now, everyone settle down. It's time for my little ones to go to sleep."

The next morning, Mother Eagle awoke early. "Be very quiet while I'm gone," she warned. "No fighting! I'll be back soon."

Off she flew to gather food for her babies.

After a short time, Ernie began
to grumble.

"I'm bored," pouted Ernie. " I'll bet I can fly from
here to the next tree faster than you can, Edgar!"

"Mother will be very angry with you," cried Ethel! "She says we should stay
here and wait for her when we want to practice flying."

"Don't be such a baby, Ethel," scoffed Ernie!. "Come on, Edgar! I'll bet I can
reach that tree before you do!"

"I don't know," Edgar said nervously. He wasn't so sure he could fly that far.

"Come on, Edgar! Are you an Eagle or a chicken? Edgar is a chicken," teased
Ernie.

"He is not," shouted Ethel! "He can fly faster and further than you can!
Go ahead, Edgar! Show him how well you can fly!"

Edgar didn't want Ethel to think he was a chicken. He was an Eagle and by golly,
he was going to prove it!

Edgar hopped up on the edge of the nest.

"Okay, Ernie. Pick a tree and we'll see who's
the best eagle," crowed Edgar!

Ernie hopped up next to Edgar.

"We'll just fly from here to the big oak tree right next to this
tree. We'll come right back and Mother will never know we
were gone," said Ernie.

"On you mark," shouted Ethel, "spread your wings....
...and...............GO!"

Edgar and Ernie spread their wings and flew out of
the nest.
Edgar squinted trying to see the big oak tree.
It seemed so much further away than it did from the
safety of the nest.

"Edgar," shouted Ernie! "You're going the wrong way!
This way, Edgar!" But, it was too late.
Edgar hadn't practiced changing directions yet.
He saw a nice tree ahead of him.

"Get ready," Edgar said out loud, "get
set.....and.....land!"

He stretched out his feet to grab the branch on
the tree and.........

SPLAT!!

Edgar crashed into something hard.
He slid down and landed on
the ground. He shook his head.

"That is one flat tree," thought Edgar.

"HA, HA! That's the funniest thing I've ever seen," laughed a squirrel.

"Who are you," squinted Edgar? "Is that you, Ernie?"

"No," laughed the squirrel. "I'm Sylvester the Squirrel.
"Watch what I can do!" He scurried up the tree
and then back down. "Can you do that," he asked Edgar?

"I don't think so," said Edgar, sadly. "I've lost my family
and I need to find them. Can you help me?"

"No problem," said Sylvester. "Just follow me."

Off he ran.

Edgar tried to follow but Sylvester ran too fast!

It wasn't long before Edgar couldn't see him anymore.

Poor Edgar! How would he ever find his family?

He was deep in the forest and all the trees looked the same.

Edgar heard a noise and squinted to see what it was.
He saw a shape moving towards him.

"Mother, is that you," he called?

"Mother," came the reply? "I thought Eagles had really good vision.
No, I'm not your Mother. My name is Foster and I'm a Fox.
Are you lost?"

"Yes," cried Edgar! "I need to find my family. I wish I could see
better. Then I could fly and see where my home is."

"Maybe you can do what I do," said Foster the Fox.
"I get really close to the ground, like this.
Then, I smell...SNIFF!!"

Edgar stuck his beak on the ground and SNIFFED!

"I smell food," cried Sylvester and off he ran.

"I don't smell anything," moaned Edgar.

Edgar heard a funny noise coming from under a shrub.
He peaked through the shrub and saw a pond.
"RRRRRRRRRRRRibet...RRRRibet......RRRRRRibet."

"Hello," called Edgar.   "Is that you, Mother?"

"RRRRRRRidiculous...RRRRRribet.   "I'm Freddie the Frog.   RRRRibet."

"Oh," sighed Edgar.   "I'm trying to find my family.
I can't see very well.   Can you help me?"

"RRRRRRRight...RRRRRight.   Follow me," croaked Freddie.
He dove into the water and disappeared.

Edgar tried to dive into the pond and came up sputtering.
"Where are you, Freddie?   I can't see you!"
But, Freddie was gone and didn't answer.

Edgar heard splashing on the other side of the pond.
"Mother," he called.   "Is that you, Mother?"

"Quack, Quack," came the reply.

"Mother, what's wrong with your voice?
Are you sick," cried Edgar?

"Oh, Dear!   Quack, Quack!   Oh, Dear!"

"What's wrong, Mother," cried Edgar?

"I'm not your Mother. Quack! I'm Dizzy Duck. Who are you?"

"I'm Edgar and I'm an Eagle. I'm trying to find my family. Can you help me?"

"Sure, just follow me," said Dizzy. Edgar jumped into the pond and followed
Dizzy. Around and around they swam.

"I think I know why they call you Dizzy," said Edgar.
"Do you know where we're going?"

"Of course," said Dizzy. "I go this way every day."

"Thank you for your help," said Edgar.
He was very dizzy as he climbed out of the pond.

"Quack....glad to help....Quack....Oh, Dear!"

Edgar walked on through the woods.
Suddenly, he heard a sound and
stopped to listen. He heard a soft
 growl.

 "Mother," shouted Edgar! "Is that you?"

A brown furry critter peaked around a tree at
Edgar "Uh, I'm not sure. Are you a bear?"

"No," said Edgar. "I'm an Eagle."

"Well, I guess I'm not your Mother, then.
I'm Bobo the Bear."

"It's nice to meet you, Bobo. I'm trying to find
my family. Can you help me?"

"Uh, I'm not sure," said Bobo. "Do you live in a
den?"

 "Is a den like a tree?"

"Oh, no," said Bobo. "But, I can climb trees. If
you can show me which tree you live in, I can
climb it." "No," Edgar said sadly. "I can't see
very well so I can't find my family tree."

   "No problem," said Bobo. "Just follow me."

Edgar followed Bobo to a tree. He heard
a loud buzzing noise.

Bobo climbed up the tree and
Edgar flew up beside him.

"I think I found your family," said Bobo.
He stuck his hand into a beehive and
pulled out a paw full of honey.

Soon, bees were swarming around Bobo and Edgar.

"Yikes," squealed Edgar! "This isn't my family!"

He flew quickly out of the tree and
ran into the forest.

"Oh, my," sighed Edgar. " It's getting dark and
I still haven't found my family."

"Your family? You're looking for your family?" A baby raccoon
waddled over to Edgar. "What happened to your family?"

"Ethel, is that you," cried Edgar?

"Oh, goodness, no! My name is Rosie and I'm a Raccoon.
What happened to your family?"

"I flew out of my nest and now I'm lost. Can you help me?"

"Oh, sure," said Rosie. "I see really well in the dark. Just as soon as
I get some dinner, you can follow me and I'll help you
find your family."

Rosie climbed into a garbage can and ate heartily.
She threw food down to Edgar so that he could eat, too.
When they were done eating, Rosie jumped down to the ground.

"Okay, let's go find your family," said Rosie.

"Wait," cried Edgar! "I can't see in the dark!"

"Uh-Oh," said Rosie. "I can't see well in the daytime. Sorry."

Off Rosie ran to find more food.

"Oh, Woe is me," cried Edgar!

"Whooooo is you," said a voice
above Edgar?

"Mother, is that you," cried Edgar?

"Whoooo, me? No, I'm an Owl and
my name is Ollie. Whooooo are you?"

"I'm Edgar the Eagle. I'm lost and so very
tired. Can you help me?"

"Whoooooooo, Me? Sure, Edgar.
Yooooou can sleep in my nest
tonight. I hunt for food at night. You
can rest in my nest
until I return in the morning."

"Oh, thank you, Ollie! After I sleep, I'm sure I'll be
able to find my family."

So, Edgar slept the night away in Ollie's nest.

The next morning, Edgar continued
his search for his family.

Scratch, Scratch, Scratch!!

"Ethel, Ernie, is that you," called Edgar?

"No," squeaked a little Chipmunk. "My name is
Chase the Chipmunk. Do you want to play Hide and Seek?"

"I don't think so," sighed Edgar. "I can't see very well."

"Why," asked Chase?

"I don't know why. Everyone else in my family can see very
well. I'm the only one who can't see very well. I've been
looking for my family for a very long time. Can you help me
find them?"

"Oh," said Chase. "I'm sorry that you're lost. I hope
you find your family soon. I'll run ahead
and see if I can find them."

"Thanks," yelled Edgar as Chase ran away.

"Meow.....Meow."

"Mother, is that you," asked Edgar?

"Oh, no," giggled the kitten. "My name is Carmen the Kitty.
Do you want to play with me?"

"Hello, Carmen," said Edgar. " I think I should
keep looking for my family."

"Are you lost," asked Carmen?

"Yes, I guess I am. I can't see very
well to find my way home,"
said Edgar sadly.

"I'm sorry you're lost. Maybe you'll feel
better if you play with me. My Mother
found a new toy on a picnic table.
She's always telling me I should share.
Here, let me show you how my
new toy works."

"Sure", sighed Edgar.

"I think you're supposed to hang them on your face like this.
It makes everything look bigger.
They don't fit me very well, though."

"Here," said Carmen. "Let me help you put these on."

"WOW" exclaimed Edgar! "I can see everything really
well with these! Oh, Carmen! I can see!"

"Yippee," shouted Carmen! "They don't fit me very well and
I get dizzy looking through them, so you can keep them, Edgar."

Suddenly, Chase the Chipmunk ran up to Edgar and Carmen.
"Edgar," shouted Chase! "There's a big bird flying around and
calling your name! I think I found your family! Follow me!"

"Oh, thank you, Chase! And thank you, Carmen," said Edgar!
"I'll never forget how you both helped me."

"You're welcome," purred Carmen.

Edgar followed Chase to an open field.
There was his Mother circling high above
calling his name.

"Thank you, Chase," cried Edgar! "I'll never forget
how kind
you and Carmen were to me."

"You're welcome," chattered Chase.
"We all need to help each other."

""You're so right," said Edgar.

And with that he soared into the sky.

Edgar had finally found his family.